"Your hair's tangled like Samson, the super-strong,
long-haired warrior who could do whatever he wanted.
Your fringe is long like Rapunzel,
the princess trapped in the tower."

Dad tells the barber to shave cool things
into the back of my head and afterwards
we joke and make up rhymes...

THE HAIRDO GOT AWAY

Joseph Coelho   Fiona Lumbers

Andersen Press

Dad takes me to the barber's once a month,
without fail, come rain or shine.
I watch my hair fall into my lap
as the barber chats.

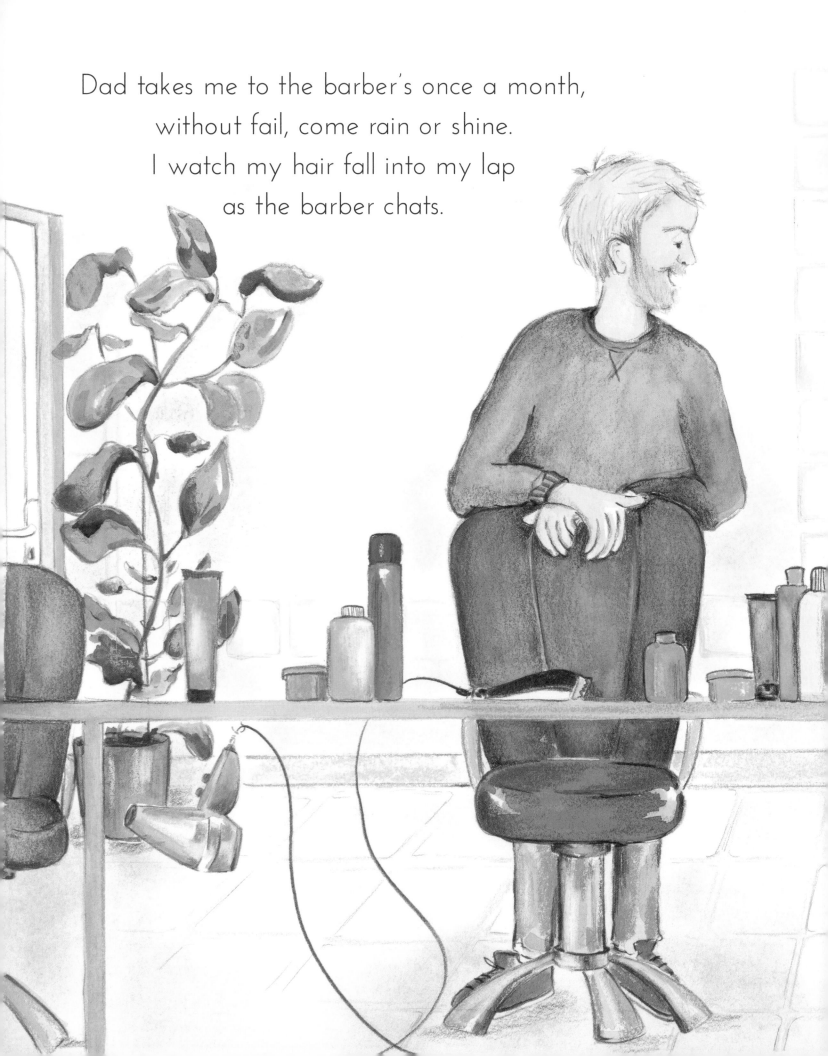

"It's an arrow to help you keep your head high!"

"Up to the sky."

"As you go around school..."

"I'm gonna look cool!"

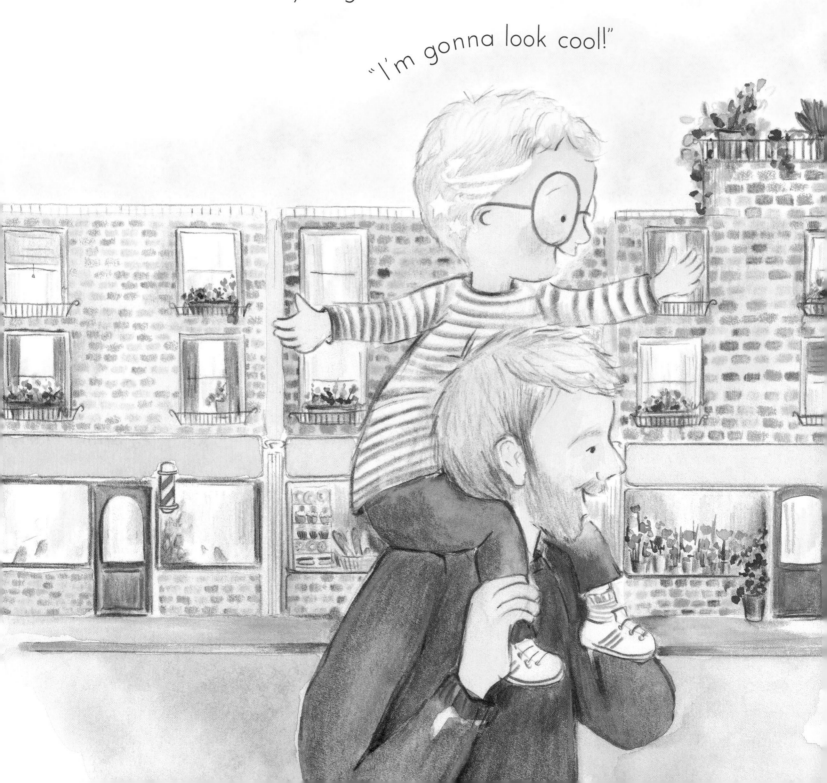

But Mum thinks the arrow on my head is not right for school.

Without hair to cover my ears I can hear everything.
So I get under my covers and imagine I'm alone in a
tower like Rapunzel or in a battle like Samson,
fighting yelling lions and shouting armies.

Days pass and my hair gets big, but, come rain or shine,
Dad doesn't come to take me to the barber's.
The arrow has gone from my head.

Weeks pass and my hair gets huge, but, come rain or shine,
Dad doesn't come to take me to the barber's.
I can't fit my hat on my head.

Months pass and my hair gets ginormous, but, come rain or shine, Dad doesn't come to take me to the barber's. There are knots inside my head.

My hair gets curly, wavy,
tangled down my back.

I disappear under my hair.

Over my ears, over my eyes.

Long at the sides.

It's been two months, four days, and eight hours since I last saw Dad. I sit in my usual seat at school.

"Who's the new kid?"

"I've never seen him - her? - before."

I am getting hot and bothered under all my hair.
Things have changed for me and everyone knows it.
Even Miss Clarke doesn't recognise me...
"New child – come to the front and introduce yourself."
"But Miss, it's me."
"Pardon? I can't understand you under all that hair."

Tomorrow is the school trip to the zoo.
Normally I'd tell Dad and he'd
give me some money.
I collect erasers and keyrings
and badges.

I need some spending money
to keep my collection going.

It's been six months, eight days and twelve hours since I last saw Dad, so I figure I better ask Mum.

But her hair is so long she can't hear me.

I'm here at the stupid zoo with no pocket money,
so no erasers or badges or keyrings for my collection.

If no one knows who I am then I might as well
be like Samson and do whatever I want!

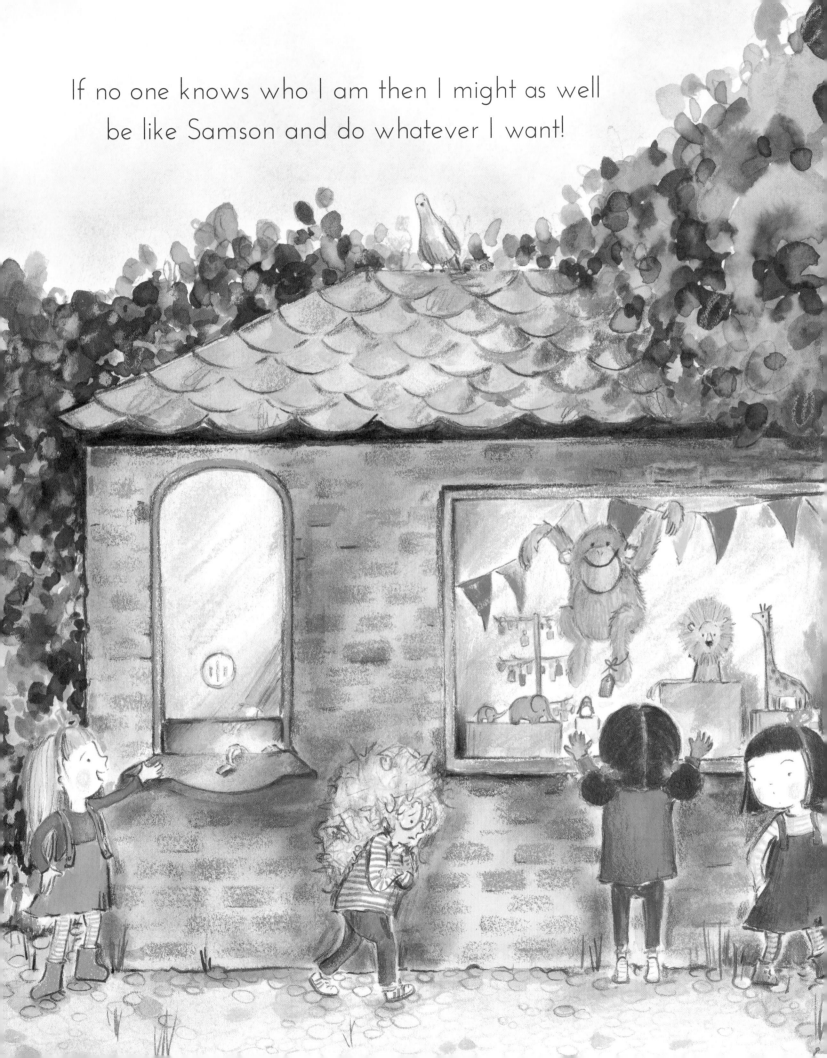

We go past the baby emus.
They squawk, they stare, they jump the fence,
they nest in my hair!

"Child, will you stop teasing the animals!" says Miss Clarke.

We pass the lions.
They mewl, they stare,
shaking their manes,
scared by my hair.

"Child, will
you STOP teasing the
animals!" shouts Miss Clarke.

We pass the buffalo.
They moo, they stare,
they bash at their pen,
they stampede everywhere.

"CHILD, WILL YOU STOP
TEASING THE ANIMALS!"
thunders Miss Clarke.

I'm in Mr Burgess's office – he's the head and he's bald.
We have to talk about my behaviour at the zoo
while everyone else is having sport.

But he doesn't tell me off – instead he gives me
a book full of stories about people with lots of hair.

There's Rapunzel: her hair grew so long a prince climbed up it. If my hair was as long as Rapunzel's Dad might use it to climb up to our flat.

And there's Samson: his hair gave him strength, but also got him in a whole lot of trouble, a bit like me.

After school I see Mum with a man covered in hair.
Curly, wavy, tangled hair down his back, over his ears,
over his eyes, long at the sides.

It's Dad!

His hair has been troublesome for him too.
His feelings got him hot and bothered and
tangled in frowns and knotted in sadness.

But all he wanted to do was come home,
and now he is back.

The three of us all get a new hairstyle.
I watch my hair fall into my lap and I feel strong like
Samson defeating an army and happy like Rapunzel
climbing down from her lonely tower.

The three of us laugh and joke
as I watch my hair fall into my lap

Tangles of sadness – snipped to smiles.
Knots of worry – trimmed to tickles.
My family – woven together.

For the teachers, who know the power a
book recommendation can hold – J.C.

For Sean – F.L.

This paperback edition first published in 2021 by Andersen Press Ltd.

First published in Great Britain in 2019 by Andersen Press Ltd.,

20 Vauxhall Bridge Road, London, SW1V 2SA, UK

Vijverlaan 48, 3062 HL Rotterdam, Nederland

Text copyright © Joseph Coelho, 2019.

Illustration copyright © Fiona Lumbers, 2019.

The rights of Joseph Coelho and Fiona Lumbers to be identified as the

author and illustrator of this work have been asserted by them in accordance

with the Copyright, Designs and Patents Act, 1988.

Printed and bound in China.

1   3   5   7   9   10   8   6   4   2

British Library Cataloguing in Publication Data available.

ISBN 978 1 78344 906 4